DISCARD

Dear Cinderella

By **Marian Moore** & **Mary Jane Kensington**
Illustrated by **Julie Olson**

Orchard Books · New York · An Imprint of Scholastic Inc.

Library of Congress Cataloging-in-Publication Data
Moore, Marian.
Dear Cinderella / by Marian Moore and Mary Jane Kensington ; illustrated by Julie Olson. — 1st ed.
p. cm.
Summary: Cinderella and Snow White exchange letters and become friends as they tell each other about
the problems they face with their stepmothers and other events in their lives.
ISBN 978-0-545-34220-9
[1. Princesses—Fiction. 2. Characters in literature—Fiction.
3.Letters—Fiction.] I. Kensington, Mary Jane. II. Olson, Julie, 1976–
ill. III. Title.
PZ7.M78712De 2012
[E]—dc22   2010052067

10 9 8 7 6 5 4 3 2 1   12 13 14 15 16

Printed in Singapore 46
First edition, February 2012

The display type was set in Belleview and Dorchester Script.
The text was set in Edwardian Medium.
The art was created using watercolor, ink, and digital media.
Book design by Chelsea C. Donaldson

For my grandmother,
for coloring with me. —M.M.

For Lukas & Olivia, who changed
our kingdom forever after. —M.J.K.

To my many, many nieces.
You are all princesses! —J.O.

Dear Cinderella,

I am so happy that we are going to be pen pals. I live in a great big castle with my mean stepmother, the queen. Even though I am a princess, she makes me work all the time. All I do is scrub the floors, wash the windows, and clean all day. I wish I lived in some faraway place where dreams come true.

I hope things are better for you.

Write back soon,
Snow White

Dear Snow White,

    Your letter made my day! Sorry to hear about your wicked stepmother. . . . I know how you feel. I live with my stepmother and my two stepsisters, who always have work for me to do.

    I don't mind working in the garden, feeding the animals, and cooking the meals. Singing and dancing when you are scrubbing, washing, and cleaning make the chores seem like fun.

La, la, la, la, la,
Cinderella

Dear Cinderella,

I have been singing and dancing ever since I read your letter. My stepmother is horrible to me, but I am hopeful that one day things will change.

I like to dream about Prince Charming riding up on his white horse and taking me away from my chores and, most of all, from my wicked stepmother. We'd go far away to his castle, and we'd live happily ever after! What's going on with you?

Your friend,

Snow

Dear Snow,

Today is the best day ever! My stepmother said I could go to the Prince's Ball. I am so excited. I can't stop singing!

Before I can go, I have to finish my chores, make dresses for my stepsisters, and make my own dress with the leftover scraps.

I should get started with sewing and polishing, and oh me, oh my — lots to do! I wish you could see me spinning around and around in excitement.

I am going to the ball!

I feel like the luckiest girl in the whole kingdom.

Love you lots,
Cinderella

Dear Cinderella,

I am sooooo happy for you! What will your dress look like? The ball is going to be so much fun!

I wish there was a prince in my kingdom so I could go to a ball. Instead, I have my stepmother, who spends her day talking to a magic mirror on her wall. She always asks it the same question: "Mirror, mirror, on the wall, who in this land is fairest of all?" And she always gets the same answer: "You, my queen, are fairest of all."

I hope you have a magical evening.

Best,
Snow

P.S. Tomorrow, my stepmother is sending me with the castle huntsman to spend the day in the woods. I won't have to do chores. Yippee!

Dear Snow,

Oh my! I have spent the entire day getting my stepsisters ready for the ball, and now they have gone without me! I am just starting on my dress, and I wonder if I will ever finish.

I am still hopeful that I can go. I am going to sing and sew until I'm done.

Love,
Cinderella

P.S. I'll write more later — wait! Something odd is happening here. . . .

Dear Cinderella,

I hope you made it to the ball!

You're not going to believe what happened to me.
Do you remember how I said in my letter that the
huntsman was taking me to the woods? Well, he told
me my stepmother had ordered him to get rid of me!

He told me not to go back to the castle, so I ran
into the woods to escape. I found a cute cottage, and
the sweet little man who lives there invited me to
stay and be safe.

I will write more soon.

Yours,

Snow

P.S. I hear lots of noise upstairs. . . .

Dear Snow,

I am so happy that you escaped from the wicked queen!
When I was getting ready for the ball, my very own fairy godmother appeared! And with a wave of her wand, she turned a pumpkin into a magnificent coach and little mice into horses. She turned my raggedy dress into the most beautiful gown ever, with sparkly glass slippers! The last thing she told me was to make sure I got home before midnight.

I went to the ball, and I even danced with the prince. Oh, Snow, he was so dreamy!

When the clock struck twelve, I ran as fast as I could down the palace stairs, and I lost one of my pretty glass slippers! But I got home just in time, and my stepmother didn't even know I had been at the ball!

With a smile,
Cinderella

Dear Cinderella,

I can't believe you danced with the prince and you have a special fairy godmother! What color was your dress? Will you see the prince again?

It turns out that I am staying with seven dwarfs. Can you believe it? They have been very kind to me. They are a bit messy, but I don't mind cleaning up after them. I love cooking for everyone and eating our meals together. I even made friends with the animals in the woods.

I am so happy for the both of us.

Best friends forever,

Snow

P.S. Did you find your glass slipper? It sounds so pretty!

Dear Snow,

My dress was pink and sparkly. I twirled and spun around all night.

Your new home sounds so nice, and I am glad you are finally safe and away from your stepmother.

You won't believe this, but the prince is searching every house in the kingdom. He is looking for the girl who lost her glass slipper. That's me! What am I going to do? I am busy making new dresses for my stepsisters to wear when the prince arrives. I wonder if he will recognize me.

Love you lots,
Cinderella

Dear Snow,

Is everything all right? I have not heard back from you.

Please let me know that everything is okay. . . . I love getting your letters, and I am starting to get worried.

Concerned,
Cinderella

Dear Cinderella,

We have heard so much about you from Snow White that we had to tell you what has happened. On our way home from work, we saw an old woman walking away from the cottage. We think it was the wicked queen in disguise! Snow was asleep on the floor, and she had bitten into an apple. We have tried everything we can, but we cannot wake her up.

We wanted to let you know why she has not replied to your recent letters. We hope to write to you soon with better news.

Sincerely,
The Seven Dwarfs

Dear Cinderella,

You must have been so worried!

The most awful thing happened. The apple I took a bite of had a sleeping spell, and it could only be broken by a special kiss.

But then the most wonderful thing happened. A prince had heard of a sleeping princess in the woods and he came to rescue me. Once he gave me a kiss, the spell was broken. I hugged all seven dwarfs good-bye, and we promised to stay in touch. My prince and I rode away on his white horse to his faraway kingdom, and I will never have to see my wicked stepmother again!

I am so happy. Dreams do come true!

Love,

Snow

Dear Snow,

Your prince has come, and so has mine! I am twirling around and around! I'm so glad you are okay!

The prince arrived at our home. After my stepsisters tried to fit their big feet into the glass slipper, the prince asked if there was anyone else in the house. My stepmother had locked me in my room. Luckily, the prince heard my footsteps upstairs.

He tried the glass slipper on my foot, and it fit. Magically, my rags turned back into the beautiful pink gown. He swept me away on his horse.

I am so happy!

You're right! Dreams really do come true.

Love,

Cinderella

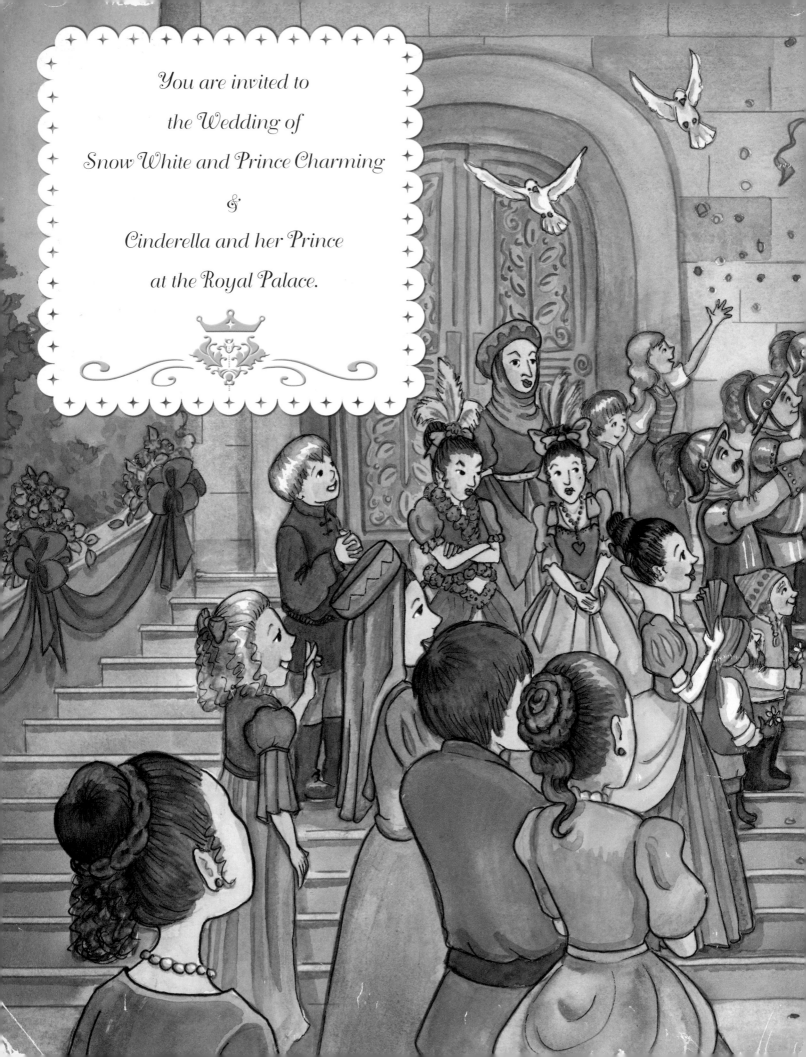

You are invited to
the Wedding of
Snow White and Prince Charming
&
Cinderella and her Prince
at the Royal Palace.

And we lived happily ever after!